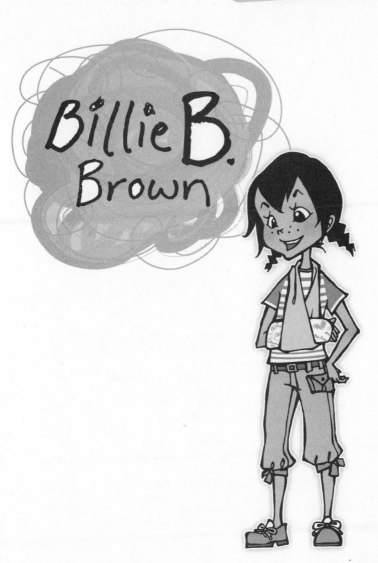

www.BillieBBrownBooks.com

Billie B. Brown Books

The Bad Butterfly
The Soccer Star
The Midnight Feast
The Second-best Friend
The Extra-special Helper
The Beautiful Haircut
The Big Sister
The Spotty Vacation
The Birthday Mix-up
The Secret Message
The Little Lie
The Best Project
The Deep End
The Copycat Kid
The Night Fright

First American Edition 2014
Kane Miller, A Division of EDC Publishing

Text copyright © 2011 Sally Rippin
Illustrations copyright © 2011 Aki Fukuoka
Logo and design copyright © 2011 Hardie Grant Egmont

First published in Australia in 2011 by Hardie Grant Egmont

For information contact:
Kane Miller, A Division of EDC Publishing
P.O. Box 470663
Tulsa, OK 74147-0663
www.kanemiller.com
www.edcpub.com
www.usbornebooksandmore.com

Library of Congress Control Number: 2013944865

Printed and bound in the United States of America
4 5 6 7 8 9 10
ISBN: 978-1-61067-257-3

The Little Lie

By Sally Rippin

Illustrated by Aki Fukuoka

Kane Miller
A DIVISION OF EDC PUBLISHING

Chapter One

Billie B. Brown has two colorful slings, three pink bandaids and a bandage around her head. Do you know what the "B" in Billie B. Brown stands for?

Broken.

Billie B. Brown has
been hunting dinosaurs
with her best friend, Jack.
A dinosaur **trampled**
all over Billie. It is a
terrible emergency!

Now Billie has two
broken arms. And maybe
a broken head, too!

One bandage

Two colorful slings

Three pink bandaids

No, not really. Billie and Jack are just playing hunters. Now Hunter Jack is pretending to bandage up Billie's broken bones.

Jack and Billie live next door to each other. They play lots of made-up games together.

"I feel much better now," says Billie.

She takes off all
the bandages. "Let's
go back out and catch
another dinosaur!"

Jack and Billie run
outside into the backyard.

Billie has a toy bow
and arrow. She shoots
the arrow up into the air.
Up, up, up it goes.

Then down, down, down.
Right onto the roof of
the shed.

"Oh no!" says Billie. "That was our last arrow!"

"Don't worry," says Jack. "We can play something else."

But Billie doesn't want to play anything else. She wants to keep playing hunters!

Billie climbs the fence to see if she can find the arrow.

The fence is very high.
Billie climbs up and up
until she is as high as
the shed roof.

"I can see the arrow!"
Billie calls down to Jack.
"It's just on the edge of
the roof. I'm sure I can
reach it."

"Be careful, Billie!" calls
Jack. He looks worried.

"Maybe we should get
your mom or dad?"

Billie leans forward, slowly, slowly, then – oh no! Billie tumbles right off the fence. **Crash!**

She lands on her arm and shouts in pain.

Jack runs over. "Are you all right, Billie?"

Billie holds her arm tight against her tummy and rocks back and forth.

She scrunches up her eyes. "**OW, OW, OW!**" she yells.

Billie's mom runs into the backyard. She bends down beside Billie. "Oh dear!" she says. "What happened?"

"I fell off the fence," wails Billie.

Her mom frowns.

"What were you doing...?
Never mind. We'd better
get you to the hospital!"

The hospital! Even though her arm hurts, Billie can't help feeling a teensy bit **excited**. It's a real emergency!

Chapter Two

Billie's mom leaves Baby Noah with Jack's mom and drives Billie straight to the hospital. A doctor takes Billie into a special room for an X-ray.

"Well," says the doctor.
"I'm afraid your arm
is broken, Billie. We'll
have to put a plaster cast
on it until it heals."

A real plaster cast and a
real sling! Billie can't wait
to show everyone at school.

Billie remembers when
Lola came to school
with a twisted ankle.
She limped around all day
and everyone wanted to sit
next to her at lunchtime.

Having a broken arm is
very **exciting**.

The next morning Billie's dad walks Billie and Jack to school. When they get there, Poppy is at the gate.

"Oh!" says Poppy. "What happened to your arm, Billie?"

"I broke it!" says Billie.

"Wow," says Poppy. "How did you do that?"

"She fell off the fence,"
says Jack.

"Cool!" says Poppy.
"I'm going to tell Ella and
Tracey!" She runs off.

Billie and Jack walk onto
the playground.

Soon Tracey, Ella and
Poppy run up to her.

"Poppy says you fell
off a fence and broke
your arm!" Ella says.

"That's right," says Billie.
She feels very **proud** that
all the girls want to see
her arm. It makes her feel
very special.

Then Billie has an idea.

She's just thought of
something that will
make *everyone* want to
be her friend.

"Actually, I was rescuing
my baby brother," Billie
says loudly.

"What?" says Jack.

Billie jabs him in the
ribs with her elbow.

"He crawled up the
fence and got stuck there,"
she says. "It was really,
really high."

"Wow!" say Poppy, Ella and Tracey. "That's amazing! Let's go and tell the others." They run off the playground.

"Tell Lola!" Billie calls out after them.

Billie turns to smile at Jack. But Jack isn't smiling.

In fact Jack doesn't look
happy at all!

Chapter Three

"What?" says Billie.

Jack frowns. "That didn't happen," he says. "You're making up stories."

"So?" says Billie. "I'm just playing a game."

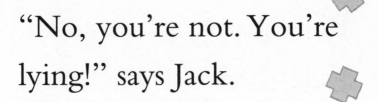

"No, you're not. You're lying!" says Jack.

Billie frowns. "Well, not really. It's just a little lie."

"It's not! A lie is a lie," says Jack.

Billie glares at Jack and Jack glares at Billie.

The girls come back with Rebecca and Lola.

"Ella says you rescued your brother and broke your arm!" says Rebecca. She is out of breath from running so fast.

"That's right," says Billie.

She doesn't look at Jack. "And also, there was a fierce dog on the other side of the fence."

The girls gasp. Billie grins **proudly**.

"Actually it was a crocodile," she says. "Our neighbors have a fierce crocodile."

Lola looks at Billie in a
funny way. "I don't believe
you," she says. "Nobody
keeps crocodiles as pets.
You're a fibber!

I bet your arm isn't
even broken!"

Lola spins around and
walks to the classroom.
The other girls follow her.

"It is! It is broken. Really
and truly!" Billie shouts
after them. "Isn't it, Jack?"

Billie looks at Jack, but
he doesn't say anything.

Then he walks away
without Billie.

Billie can't believe it.
Having a broken arm
was meant to make
Billie the most popular
girl in school!

And now even her best
friend won't talk to her.

Billie sits down under
the big pepper tree. She
feels **terrible**. Her arm
hurts and her tummy
hurts. She wants to go
home.

All Billie wanted was
for everyone to sit next
to her at lunchtime.

All she wanted was for everyone to sign her cast. Now nobody will want to sit next to her and nobody will sign her cast.

Billie B. Brown is lots of things. She is bold and bouncy. Sometimes she is even a teensy bit bossy.

But most of all, Billie B. Brown is brave. She knows what she has to do. She takes a big breath and walks into class.

What do you think she is going to do?

Chapter Four

When Billie walks
into class, everyone is
sitting on the floor in
front of Ms. Walton.
Show-and-tell is just
about to start.

"My goodness, Billie," says Ms. Walton. "It looks like you have something very special for show-and-tell this morning. Would you like to go first?"

Billie nods and walks up to the front of the class. Her heart is beating very fast.

"Um, yesterday I broke my arm," Billie says.

She points at
her arm.

"I can see that,"
Ms. Walton says.
"How did it
happen, Billie?"

Billie feels her cheeks
get **hot**. She looks at Jack.
He looks away. "Um, I fell
off the fence," she says in a
little voice.

"I was trying to get an arrow down from the shed roof."

Billie hears Lola giggle.

"Oh dear," Ms. Walton says. "You'll have to be more careful next time, won't you? Are there any questions for Billie?"

Lola is the first to stick up her hand.

"I thought you were rescuing your brother from crocodiles," she says. Some of the girls giggle.

Billie takes another deep breath.

She sees Jack watching
her. Her tummy is jumping
around **nervously**, but
she doesn't stop. "I was
just making up stories,"
she says. "I thought
it would sound more
exciting that way."

Ms. Walton smiles. "You
obviously have a very
good imagination, Billie.

Perhaps you could write a story. Any more questions?"

Rebecca jabs her hand into the air.

"Yes, Rebecca?" Ms. Walton says.

"Can I sign your cast, Billie?" says Rebecca.

"Me too!" says Poppy.

"Me too!" says Ella.

"All right, girls, settle down," Ms. Walton says. "You will all have plenty of time to sign Billie's cast at lunchtime.

Thank you, Billie.

You can sit down now."

Billie smiles. She feels
happy again. Everyone
will want to sit next to
her at lunchtime now!

But at the moment
there is only one person
she wants to sit next to.
Billie looks toward Jack.

He has a big smile on his face. Best of all, he has wriggled over to make room for Billie. Right next to him.

Collect them all!

The Bad Butterfly
By Sally Rippin

The Soccer Star
By Sally Rippin

The Midnight Feast
By Sally Rippin

The Second-best Friend
By Sally Rippin

The Extra-special Helper
By Sally Rippin

The Beautiful Haircut
By Sally Rippin

The Big Sister
By Sally Rippin

The Spotty Vacation
By Sally Rippin

The Birthday Mix-up
By Sally Rippin

The Secret Message
By Sally Rippin

The Little Lie
By Sally Rippin

The Best Project
By Sally Rippin

The Deep End
By Sally Rippin

The Copycat Kid
By Sally Rippin

The Night Fright
By Sally Rippin